P9-AOY-542

This book

belongs to:

ABBE

THE
ADVENTURES
of
ABDI

BY

MADONNA

ART BY
OLGA DUGINA AND ANDREJ DUGIN

CALLAWAY
NEW YORK
2004

Long ago, in a land far away from the one we know, where sand and mountains stretched as far as the eye could see, and snake charmers wandered the streets, there lived a little boy named Abdi. Abdi was an orphan who was looked after by an old family friend named Eli, who owned a jewelry shop. Eli was no ordinary jeweler. People came to him from near and far to have their precious gems made into exquisite necklaces, rings, and bracelets. It was said that Eli possessed magical powers, since every person who purchased or was given one of his unique ornaments was blessed with good fortune.

It was Abdi's job to greet the customers, serve them mint tea, and sweep the floor at the end of the day. There were two simple rooms at the back of the shop where Abdi and Eli shared their meals and slept.

Eli taught Abdi many things—how to navigate by the stars, how to make lentil soup, and most important, how to be happy. Eli was a great teacher, and Abdi was an eager student. They were the best of friends.

One day, a very important-looking man came into the shop. He wore a fancy turban and a pair of gold slippers with bells that rang when he walked.

Eli smiled at his customer and said, "How can I help you, sir?"

"I am Habib," the man with the fancy slippers announced with pride. "I have been sent by the king to commission a necklace for the queen. Word has reached the palace that you are a jeweler of many talents."

With that, he unrolled a large scroll, and on it was a picture of a very grand-looking necklace made of precious stones. The old man nodded and said nothing.

"It must shine like the sun and move like a snake," demanded Habib in a very bossy voice.

Eli raised an eyebrow, but still he said nothing.

Habib carried on, "I will return in four weeks to bring it to the king."

Eli looked at Abdi, and they smiled at each other—they knew that such a necklace would be impossible to make in such a short time.

At last, he spoke to Habib, "Everything I make is made with love and takes time. I will need much longer than four weeks."

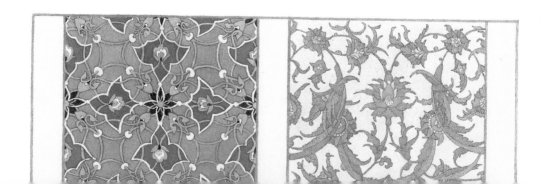

To this Habib replied, "Four weeks is all the time that you have, for then it will be the queen's birthday. I'm sure you would not want to disappoint the king. I shall leave you this as a deposit."

The man pulled out a big purse from his silk jacket and dropped it onto the counter. Then he spun round on his fancy shoes and walked out of the shop.

The old man turned to the boy and said, "We are going to have to work very hard, Abdi."

"We?" asked Abdi.

"Yes, we. I cannot do a job like this on my own. I will need your help," said Eli.

But Abdi knew that it was not possible for the old man to make the necklace in the time he was given. He had watched him carefully over the years, and he was sure that it would take much longer to make something so splendid.

He tried to reason with Eli. "We will not be able to do it. It is too much work. You will end up disappointing the king, and he will put us both in prison."

The old man held up his hand and said, "This is the job that we have been given. We have no other choice, so we must be certain that we can do it. And remember that everything we have been given in life is always for the best. Do you understand?"

Abdi had learned many lessons from Eli already, and he had never steered him wrong, so he knew he must be right.

Abdi nodded and replied, "Yes, I understand."

So day and night the old man worked, and day and night Abdi held his tools for him, brought him his meals, and kept the shop tidy. They had time for only a few hours of sleep each night before having to start work again the next day. The weeks passed. Eventually, the day arrived when the necklace was to be collected.

$\mathcal{E}$li held up his masterpiece at last, and Abdi saw that it glistened in the sunlight and moved like a snake. Its golden clasp was made in the shape of a snake's head, and best of all, it had a tongue made of diamonds that wriggled in and out of its mouth. Eli was pleased, and even though he was very tired, he still managed to smile.

"I cannot believe you finished it in time!" exclaimed Abdi.

And the old man replied, "I was certain it was for the best. Without certainty, we can accomplish nothing."

At that very moment, the postman arrived with a letter for Eli. He could tell it was an important letter, because there was a big crown on the envelope. The postman was very excited—it was rare to receive a royal letter in the village. Eli gave it to the boy and asked him to open it.

Abdi read it out loud. "Due to unforeseen circumstances, you have been summoned to bring the necklace to the king before the queen's birthday. You must come at once."

The old man did not look worried.

"When is the queen's birthday?" he asked.

"The day after tomorrow," replied the postman.

"What are you going to do?" asked Abdi. "You have not slept in a month, and you will never get there in time!"

And Eli replied, "Do you not see, Abdi? This is just another test, and you must recognize it as such. You must say to yourself, 'I am sure it is for the best!' You must have certainty."

"But what will happen if you do not make it to the palace in time?" asked Abdi.

Eli smiled and said, "But it is you who will be going."

Naturally Abdi was frightened by such a journey, but he remembered what Eli had said to him again and again, and he thought, "I am sure it is for the best!"

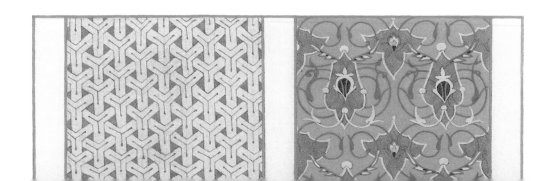

So Abdi set off with the precious necklace wrapped in silk and sealed in a box. Eli had made sure he would have enough food and water for the long journey through the desert. Abdi was lucky to catch a ride with a caravan of Bedouins traveling in the same direction. The travelers were very friendly and made him feel welcome. They sang songs, and Abdi shared his bread and sweets.

Two rather noisy fellows named El Shaydi and Ratib rode alongside Abdi, asking all kinds of questions. They wanted to know where Abdi was going and what he was carrying. They laughed rather a lot and kept slapping each other on the back. But because Abdi felt so comfortable, he told them all about the special necklace he was carrying to the queen.

When night came, the camel train stopped and everyone pitched tents. Soon Abdi fell asleep under the stars with his precious cargo lying next to him. El Shaydi and Ratib crept up to him as quiet as mice to search his bag. When they found the necklace wrapped in silk, they could not believe their eyes. They took it and stuffed it into their bag, and as they did, they saw a small snake slithering by.

El Shaydi, being the not-too-clever scoundrel that he was, thought it would be funny to replace the necklace with the snake.

Ratib cackled with excitement, "Shaydi, Shaydi, a pretty necklace for the lady!"

"Quiet, you idiot. Speak when you are spoken to," hissed El Shaydi, and off they went into the night, leaving the caravan behind.

When Abdi awoke, he made sure the box was still in his bag. And all seemed well.

Hours later, Abdi arrived at the palace. Many guards stood in front of the gate. One was very tall and carried many large swords.

Abdi stepped forward to speak to him, and in a timid voice he said, "I am here to see the king."

The guard tipped his head back at the sky and laughed. And when he looked down, he said in a very deep voice, "And why would the king want to see you?"

To this Abdi replied, "I have brought a very special necklace for the queen."

There was a great murmuring among the guards, and the tall one disappeared for what seemed like an eternity. Abdi hopped from foot to foot, anxious to deliver the gift and even more anxious to find a bathroom. Finally, the guard returned, and Abdi was allowed to enter the palace gates.

"They were not expecting a boy," grumbled the guard. "Follow me."

*A*bdi entered the palace and could not believe his eyes. There was a large courtyard inlaid with gold, and in the center was a shallow pool where tall pink birds stood on one leg. Children splashed around the edges of the pool laughing and playing, and no one shouted at them. Servants scurried around carrying large platters of delicious-looking fruit. On a beautifully woven rug in the middle of the room sat a lovely girl playing a lute and singing songs that Abdi had never heard before. He could not take his eyes off her.

"Keep up," barked the guard.

Everything Abdi saw made his head turn. Finally, they reached a big door. The guard asked him to wait, and once again, he disappeared. Abdi looked up and saw small furry animals with big eyes hanging from the ceiling. Just as he was about to run and find a bathroom, the guard returned and announced, "The king wishes to see you."

Abdi gulped. He had not thought that he was actually going to meet the king. He was very nervous.

"But," he said to himself, "I am sure it is all for the best."

Abdi entered a large room that looked as if it had been dipped in gold. He approached the throne.

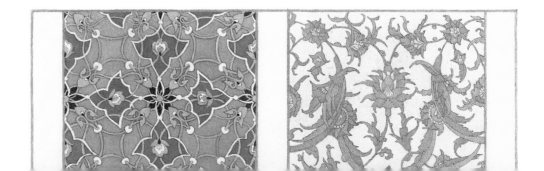

The king looked at the little boy and frowned. "Who might you be? And where is the jeweler? Did he not want to meet the king?"

The king sounded very grumpy, but Abdi spoke up. "My name is Abdi, Your Majesty. It is not what you think. The jeweler is an old man, and he has not slept in weeks, because he has been working so hard to make your necklace in time. He was not strong enough to travel the long distance, so I have brought the gift instead."

"Well, bring it forth, and be quick about it," commanded the king.

Abdi placed the gift at the foot of the throne, and a servant of the king knelt to hand it to him. The king opened the box and a snake fell out onto his lap.

"What sort of trickery is this?" the king shouted, dropping the snake to the floor.

Abdi was in shock. He tried to explain, "I do not know what happened, Your Majesty. When I left my village, I was carrying the most beautiful necklace in the world."

"Arrest the boy and throw him in the dungeon. And let him keep his precious gift," shouted the king as he stormed out of the great hall.

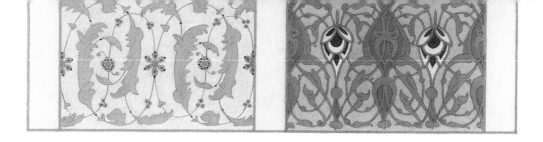

Abdi could feel fear rising up within him. But he remembered what Eli had taught him: No matter how bad things might seem, he had to believe that it was all for the best. Abdi held on tight to this advice. But the guards still threw him into the dungeon.

Abdi tried to look on the bright side and remain positive. At least now he could go to the bathroom.

One whole week went by, and poor Abdi had nothing to eat or drink except a few scraps of hard bread and some dirty water. What little he had, he shared with the snake, who became a very good friend.

Not every snake is a snake in the grass, you know.

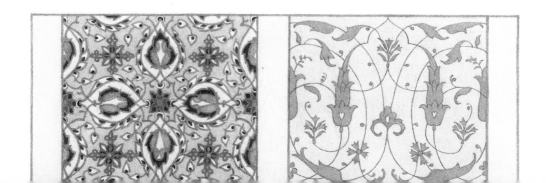

Suddenly, Abdi heard the key turning in the lock and a familiar voice coming from the other side. The door opened, and there stood Eli, with a twinkle in his eye.

"Are you all right, my son?" he asked.

"Yes," replied Abdi, "and very happy to see you."

Eli embraced him and whispered in his ear, "Good, because we are going to see the king. Now, where is your snake?"

Abdi went over to the corner of his cell and picked up his new friend, who was coiled around himself to keep warm. Outside, the guards waited impatiently to take them to the king.

When they were led into the great hall, Abdi could feel a mixture of anger and fear in the air, but Eli did not seem bothered, so Abdi decided to ignore it.

The king sat on his throne next to the queen and spoke to Eli. "I had heard that you were the best jeweler in the land. That is why I entrusted you with this royal task. And you have the impudence to send me a boy with a snake."

To this the old man replied, "A thousand pardons, Your Majesty, but what the boy has brought you only appears to be a snake. If you place it on your good queen's neck, you shall find that it is, in fact, a necklace."

"Do not mock me!" shouted the king.

Eli tried to reassure him. "The snake is not poisonous, Your Majesty, and I swear to you that no harm could come to Her Royal Highness."

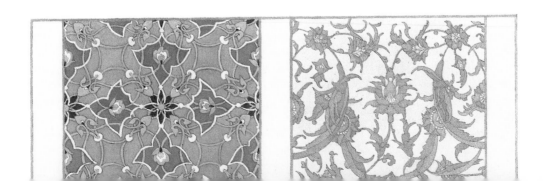

T he queen, who was sometimes braver than the king, looked at Eli and smiled. "I would like to try it on," she said in a very calm voice.

The king looked surprised, but he did not want to upset his wife, so he nodded to the old man to obey the queen's wishes.

The queen stood up, and Eli walked behind her to place the snake around her neck. In an instant, the snake turned into a brilliant and blinding strand of the most exquisite diamonds and rubies that Abdi had ever seen. The clasp was a snake's head made of gold, with a tongue made of diamonds that wriggled in and out of its mouth. The queen was overcome with joy.

"I have never seen anything so lovely. What a wonderful birthday gift," she said, as she ran to kiss the king, who was now so surprised he could hardly speak—but also very happy.

"You have done well—very well, indeed!" the king exclaimed to Eli, admiring the queen's neck and the smile on her face. "You shall be greatly rewarded."

mmediately, a box of gold coins and jewels was brought forth for Eli and Abdi, and soon they were sent on their way. This time, Abdi made sure he went to the bathroom first.

They traveled home by caravan, the same way Abdi had come. Abdi wanted to ask Eli so many questions, but before he had a chance, the old man spoke. "The power of certainty is without limits. In life, there will be many tests you will have to face. You must hold on to the belief that everything that happens is for the best."

Soon night fell, and the caravan stopped to pitch their tents and rest until morning. Eli fell asleep, but Abdi stayed awake, thinking about what the old man had said. He felt the presence of someone behind him and turned to see the men he had befriended on his trip to the palace—shady El Shaydi and old

Ratib. They were wearing new clothes and some smelly perfume.

"Fancy meeting you here," said El Shaydi, in his most pretend-friendly voice.

"Yes, fancy that!" echoed Ratib, for he never had any ideas of his own.

The men tried not to look surprised as Abdi told them everything that had happened—how he had given the king a snake that had turned into a necklace, and how the king had rewarded him with gold. El Shaydi and the Rat-man thought it was the best story ever. They rolled around in the dirt for ages, laughing and tearing their new clothes.

Finally, El Shadyi decided there was no time to lose. He slapped Ratib on the back of his head, and they ran off in a flurry of dust. Two days later, they arrived at the palace, with a large bag of snakes, begging to see the king.

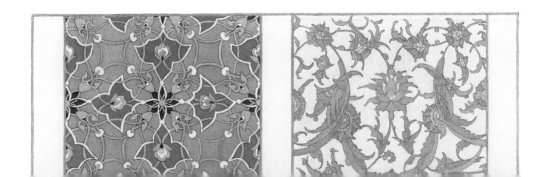

When they were granted an audience, they threw the bag open at the king's feet. But the snakes did nothing but slither around and frighten the poor queen. Needless to say, the king was not pleased. He ordered the men and their bag of snakes to be thrown into the dungeon, where they would live on hard crusts of bread and dirty water for a very long time. The snakes were not impressed, and they did not hang around for very long.

As for Abdi, he continued to study and learn from Eli, and in time he, too, became a very fine jeweler. Of that, I am certain.

Produced and published by
CALLAWAY EDITIONS
54 Seventh Avenue South
New York, New York 10014

A division of
CALLAWAY
ARTS & ENTERTAINMENT

Nicholas Callaway, President and Publisher
Antoinette White, Senior Editor • Toshiya Masuda, Art Director
George Gould, Production Director • Joya Rajadhyaksha, Associate Editor
Ivan Wong, Jr. and José Rodríguez, Production • Sofia Dumery, Design
Amy Cloud, Assistant Editor • Katy Leibold, Publishing Assistant • Krupa Jhaveri, Design Assistant
Kathryn Bradwell, Executive Assistant to the Publisher

Copyright © 2004 by Madonna
All rights reserved. No part of this publication may be reproduced, or stored in a retrieval system,
or transmitted in any form or by any means, electronic, mechanical, photocopying, recording,
or otherwise, without written permission of the publisher.

Distributed in the United States by Viking Children's Books.

Callaway Arts & Entertainment, the Callaway logotype, and Callaway Editions, Inc., are trademarks.

ISBN 0-670-05889-0

Library of Congress Cataloging-in-Publication Data available upon request.

10 9 8 7 6 5 4 3 2 1   04 05 06 07 08 09 10

Printed in the United States of America

Visit Madonna at www.madonna.com   Visit Callaway at www.callaway.com

All of Madonna's proceeds from this book will be donated to the Spirituality for Kids Foundation.

MADONNA RITCHIE has had many adventures of her own in her varied and successful career as
a musician, actress, and author. She has sold two hundred million albums worldwide, appeared in 18 movies,
and released three best-selling children's books—*The English Roses*, *Mr. Peabody's Apples*, and *Yakov and the Seven
Thieves*—in 40 languages and more than 100 countries. She lives with her husband, movie director Guy Ritchie,
and her two children, Lola and Rocco, in London and Los Angeles.

OLGA DUGINA AND ANDREJ DUGIN met and were married in Moscow, where she was his art student. They
have been living in Germany since 1989, working as illustrators on book and film projects, including *Harry Potter
and the Prisoner of Azkaban*, and also teaching art. This is their fourth picture book.

A NOTE ON THE TYPE:

This book is set in Diotima, designed by Gudrun Zapf von Hesse in 1948. It is named after Diotima of Mantinea,
the earliest recorded woman philosopher, who is said to have taught Socrates.

FIRST EDITION